It's Monday. A sunny morning in June. I leave my office. I'm going to the First City Bank on Sunset Boulevard. I feel good. I finished a job last week and they paid me $5000. I'm going to put the money in the bank.

Outside the bank I see a woman with long blonde hair. I smile at her. She looks away and walks down the street.

Then I get a big surprise. I see a duck! The duck is coming out of the bank. In fact, it's someone with a duck's face. It's someone with a duck mask on. The duck has a brown bag in its left hand. In its right hand the duck has a gun!

I throw myself to the ground. The duck runs past me. A motorbike engine starts. I look up. No duck. And no blonde woman. The motorbike is a long way down the street.

I stand up and I look at my clothes. My new grey suit is dirty. I decide to go home. I'm not going to put my money in the First City Bank.

Then I hear a police car. It stops outside the bank. More police cars come. A policeman walks up to me.

'Did you see the bank robber?' the policeman asks.

'Yes,' I reply. 'It was a duck!'

President Carter

The police ask me questions for three hours. Then I drive back to my office. The car radio is on.

This is the two o'clock news. $10 000 000 was stolen from the First City Bank on Sunset Boulevard this morning. The raider escaped on a motorbike.

When I get to my office I sit down. I put my feet on the desk. I don't know what to do. Perhaps I'll put my money in another bank. Perhaps I'll have a holiday. Perhaps I'll have a short rest. I close my eyes and fall asleep.

The telephone rings and wakes me up. I answer it.

'This is Ronald Carter,' says a deep voice. 'I'm the President of the First City Bank. We don't know each other but …'

'Hello, Mr Carter,' I say. 'Thank you for calling me. But I'm not going to put my money in your bank …'

'Shut up, Samuel, and listen!' Carter shouts. 'I don't want your money. I want you. I want you to work for me. I need a private detective. Come and see me now!'

Carter tells me where his office is. I drive across town. The headquarters of the First City Bank is in a tall office building. There is a private car park. The car park is full. Then I see a sign. The sign says: President Only. I park my old grey Chrysler by the sign.

I go into the building and get into the elevator. I ride up to the tenth floor. A secretary takes me to Carter's office. I go in. It's a very big room. Everything is white. The walls are white. The furniture is white. There is a thick white carpet. The carpet is so thick that it covers my shoes. I walk across the carpet to the desk. Bank President Carter is sitting at the desk. He has white hair and a white moustache. He looks very unhappy. He has lost $10 000 000. Of course, he's an unhappy man.

We shake hands. Carter doesn't ask me to sit down. There is silence. Carter looks at me. I wait.

9

Carter doesn't laugh.

'Listen,' he says. 'The bank is in trouble. There were five robberies last week. We lost $150 000 000. Today's raider took $10 000 000. There mustn't be any more robberies. People don't want to put their money in the bank now.'

'I know what you mean,' I reply with a smile.

'I don't want to lose my job,' says Carter. 'The police investigation is very slow. I want you to find the robber. You can stop the raids. Help me. Help me to keep my job. The police don't know who the robber is.'

'I know,' I say with a big smile. 'I saw the robbery this morning. The robber is a duck.'

Carter is angry. 'That's not funny, Samuel. Do you want the job or not?'

'I don't know. Tell me about the other robberies,' I reply.

'Sit down,' says Carter. 'It's a long story. There were five robberies at different branches of our bank last week.'

Five Raids

MONDAY
'On Monday night, someone raided the First City Bank in Glendale Boulevard. The bank robber dug a tunnel to the bank. He made a hole in the floor of the bank. Then the robber took the money away through the tunnel.'

TUESDAY

'On Tuesday evening, a helicopter flew over our bank in Main Street. The raider came down a rope from the helicopter. He made a hole in the roof. Then he climbed down into the bank and robbed it. The raider got hold of the rope again. Then the helicopter lifted him out through the roof.'

WEDNESDAY

'On Wednesday morning, there was a raid at the First City Bank in Santa Monica. The robber stopped one of the bank's vans. The van was full of money. The robber didn't hurt the driver of the van. But he stole all the money.'

THURSDAY

'On Thursday night, the raid was at the bank on Seventh Street. First, the robber stole a big excavator. Then he drove the excavator through the glass doors of the bank. The excavator picked up a cash machine and drove off. There was a lot of money in the cash machine. The police found the excavator ten minutes later. The cash machine was empty and the robber had gone.'

SATURDAY

'On Saturday morning, one of our vans left L.A. airport. The van was going towards the city centre. The van was carrying gold. A police car stopped the van near Florence. But it was not a real police car. The bank robber was driving the car. The robber had a gun. He made the van driver get out. The robber drove off in the van with the gold.'

4

It's a Woman!

'The police don't know what to do. Every raid is different. I'll pay you $10 000. Please help me,' Carter says.

I look at Carter. I don't like him. And I don't know how to stop the robberies. I think the bank robbers are cleverer than me. And they're much cleverer than Bank President Carter. In fact, I admire the robbers!

'OK,' I reply. 'I'll help you. Can I have the addresses of all the First City Banks and a map?'

I get into the Chrysler and drive around all evening. I don't have a plan. I don't know what to do. Nothing happens. There are no bank robberies. I don't see any more ducks. At midnight I go to bed.

I get up early on Tuesday morning. I decide to watch the banks in the city centre. I park the car and walk. I walk from bank to bank. Nothing happens.

It's midday. I'm tired and I want to sit down. I decide to learn more about banks. I'll ask a bank manager about how a bank works. I walk into the First City Bank near the City Hall. I ask to see the manager. I wait outside the manager's office.

There are a lot of people in the bank. The bank manager's office door is closed. The manager's name is on the door: F. RIVERA. I can see someone in the office through the glass door.

The door opens. A woman with long blonde hair comes out. I look at her and smile. She looks away. She is carrying a plastic shopping bag. She walks to the glass front doors of the bank and leaves. I watch her. I know her face. Where have I seen her before?

I wait for five minutes. Nothing happens. At last, the secretary goes to the bank manager's door. She knocks on the door. There is no answer. She knocks again. She opens the door and screams. I run into the office. A man is sitting at the desk. His hands and legs are tied with rope. There is tape over his mouth. The safe in the corner of the office is open.

'Mr Rivera?' I ask.

The man nods. I take the tape off his mouth.

'What happened?' I ask.

'A woman came to see me,' Mr Rivera says. 'Her name was Miss Waterbird. She wanted to put some papers in the safe. She was very nice and friendly. But when I opened the safe she took a gun out of her pocket!'

'How much money was in the safe?' I ask.

'There was no money,' he replies. 'But there were lots of important papers.'

I telephone the police. I telephone Mr Carter.

'What!' Mr Carter shouts. 'You saw the robber! And the robber escaped? You did nothing?'

'Well,' I reply. 'I did find out that the robber is a woman.'

5

Under Arrest

On Wednesday, I study the map of L.A. I decide to spend the morning in Inglewood. Nothing happens.

At two o'clock on Wednesday afternoon I'm sitting in my car. It's parked outside the First City Bank in Florence Avenue. I'm drinking cola and eating a large burger. A bank van stops outside the bank. The van parks close to the bank door. I watch and eat.

A guard gets out of the van. He is carrying a heavy bag of money. Suddenly, I hear a motorbike. The motorbike drives between the van and the bank. There are two people on the motorbike. They are both wearing duck masks!

The motorbike stops by the guard. The passenger on the motorbike takes the money bag. There is a chain from the bag to the guard's wrist. The passenger cuts the chain.

I get out of the car and run to the bank. The motorbike drives straight at me. Then it turns up the road. I run back to my car and I follow the motorbike.

We drive fast along the busy streets. We come to some traffic lights. The lights are red but the motorbike does not stop. I follow. Soon I'm close to the motorbike. The passenger looks round at me.

Then I hear a police car. The car is close behind me. The car is flashing its lights. Good. Now the police can catch the robbers! The police car goes past me. I smile at the policeman and point at the motorbike. But the police car suddenly stops in front of me. I stop too.

The policeman takes me to the police station. I tell him everything.

The police telephone Mr Carter, then they let me go. I telephone Mr Carter. He is very angry.

'You saw the robbers again! Why didn't you stop them?' Carter shouts. 'Why didn't you finish the job?'

'I don't know about finishing the job,' I say. 'But I didn't finish my burger!'

6

Hands Up!

On Thursday evening, I study the map again. There hasn't been a raid on Hollywood Boulevard yet. So I spend Friday on Hollywood Boulevard. I sit in the Chrysler near the First City Bank. Nothing happens. I telephone Mr Carter in the afternoon.

I say, 'There hasn't been a raid on the bank on Hollywood Boulevard. But I think there will be a raid there soon. Can I stay in the bank tonight?'

Carter says yes. He telephones the Hollywood Boulevard bank manager. I go to the bank and stay there after it closes. The people who work in the bank go home. I sit in a chair and wait. The lights are off and it's dark. Nothing happens. I keep my eyes open.

At two o'clock in the morning, I hear a noise. I listen. My gun is in my hand. The noise is coming from the ceiling. The robbers are making a hole in the ceiling. Soon the hole is quite big.

Then someone climbs down a rope into the bank. I don't move. The robber goes to the big bank safe. The robber puts something against the safe door, then he moves away quickly. The robber is going to open the safe. There is a loud bang. There is smoke everywhere. The big safe door opens slowly.

The robber goes into the safe. A minute later, the robber comes out again with some bags. I wait. The robber ties the bags to the rope.

I walk quietly over. I point my gun at the robber.

'Hands up!' I say. I turn the light on. The robber is wearing a duck mask. I pull the mask off. It's the blonde woman. It's the same woman I have seen before. I smile. This time she smiles at me. I point to the hole in the ceiling.

Suddenly, something falls on me from the hole. It's the other robber! I drop the gun and I fall to the floor. Everything goes black.

———

When I wake up, I hear a bell ringing. Then I hear police cars. I can't move my hands. I can't see. There is something on my face.

'The robber is waking up,' a voice says.

A hand takes something off my face. I can see. There are lots of police in the bank. There is a police-woman in front of me. She is holding a duck mask in her hand. I'm lying on the floor near the empty safe. My hands are tied with rope.

'I'm not a robber,' I say. 'I'm a private detective.'

7
Twins

The policewoman in the bank does not believe me. She takes me to the police station. She asks me a lot of questions, then she locks me in a room. I wait. The door opens. Mr Carter comes in. He is very, very angry.

'The robbers escaped again! You didn't stop them,' Carter shouts. 'You're not working for me any more. You're not working for anyone. The police won't let you work. You're not a private detective now!'

Carter leaves the room. The police keep me in the room until the morning. Then they ask me more questions. At midday, the Chief of Police comes to see me.

You can go, Samuel. But you can't work as a detective. Find another job. Or leave town!

On my way to the office I buy some newspapers. I'm famous. On the front of one paper it says:

Another paper says:

I sit at my desk in the office. I look at the newspapers. I'm very tired. My head hurts. I'm hungry and thirsty. And I have no job. I put my hands over my face and I close my eyes.

'Surprise! Surprise!'

I open my eyes. Two people in duck masks are standing in my office. It's the bank robbers! One of the robbers takes off his mask. But it's not a man. It's the blonde woman. The other robber takes off his mask. It's another woman! Both women look the same. They're twins.

'Hello, Mr Samuel,' the first woman says. 'My name's Lyn.'

'And I'm her sister, Liz,' the other woman says. 'We're the bank robbers.'

Both women smile. I don't know what to say. Am I asleep? Am I dreaming?

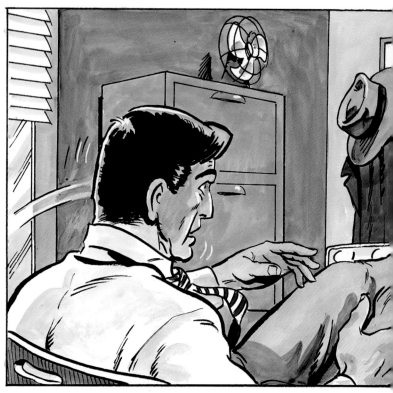

'We read about you in the newspapers,' Liz says. 'We're sorry for you. You can't work as a detective because of us. We want to help you.'

'Yes,' Lyn says. 'We want to tell you about the bank

raids. We're not robbing banks for ourselves. And we don't keep the bank's money.

'We're working for someone. He pays us $1 000 000 for each robbery. We enjoy robbing banks. We're the best bank robbers in the country.'

'I agree with you,' I reply. 'I couldn't catch you, and

I'm the best detective in the country!'

Liz laughs. 'I know why you couldn't catch us,' she says. 'We always knew where you were.'

'But how did you know where I was?' I ask.

'We knew because Carter told us,' Liz says. 'We're working for Carter!'

'Carter is robbing his own bank?' I shout. 'Are you joking?'

'No,' says Liz. 'He pays us to rob the banks. He tells us which bank to raid. He tells us where the money is. He tells us where you are. He doesn't want you to stop us. He's very rich now. He's going to leave L.A. soon.'

'But we don't like Carter,' Lyn says. 'And we're sorry for you. So we're not going to rob any more banks in L.A. We're leaving town today. We're going to Hawaii.'

Lyn gives me an envelope. 'Take this letter to the police. The letter tells them about Carter and the bank robberies. After they have read the letter, the police will let you work again.'

I close my eyes. Am I dreaming? I open my eyes. The two beautiful women are still there! Both women kiss me quickly, then they leave.

I take the letter to the police. Carter is arrested. I'm a detective again.

———

A week later I get a phone call. I put some clothes into a suitcase and get into the Chrysler. I'm going on holiday. The phone call was from Hawaii! I'm leaving town!

Published by Macmillan Heinemann ELT
Between Towns Road, Oxford OX4 3PP
Macmillan Heinemann ELT is an imprint of
Macmillan Publishers Limited
Companies and representatives throughout the world

ISBN 0 435 271822

Illustrated by John Ricardson
Cover by Mark Oldroyd and Threefold Design

Printed in China

2006 2005 2004 2003 2002
16 15 14 13 12 11 10 9 8 7